SCHOLASTIC INC.
New York Toronto London Auckland Sydney Tokyo

# THE GET ALONG GANG AND THE CHRISTMAS THIEF

By ALICE PARKER

Illustrated by NEAL McPHEETERS

ISBN 0-590-33372-0

Copyright © 1984 by American Greetings Corp. All rights reserved. Published by Scholastic Inc.

12  11  10  9  8  7  6  5  4  3  2  1      11      4  5  6  7  8  9/8

Printed in the U.S.A.                           10

It was the day before Christmas. Snow was falling in Green Meadow. The Get Along Gang was at the clubhouse caboose making final plans for their Annual Christmas Pageant.

"All right, gang," said Montgomery Moose. "Let's go over the committee reports just to make sure that everything is all set for the pageant tonight. Woolma, you're first."

"I'm going to open the show with my Sugar Plum fairy number and dance around Santa's sleigh. Then I am going to curtsey, like this and like this and like this."

"Boo," shouted Rocco.

"Shhh," said Dotty.

"How rude he is," said Lolly.

"Everyone settle down," said Montgomery. "We'll run down the list of the cast quickly. If you have learned your part, just say yes. And no comments, please."

"Santa?"
"Yes," said Rudyard.
"Mrs. Santa?"
"Yes," said Dotty.
"The elf?"
"Yes," said Portia.
"Santa's helpers?"
"Yes," said Lolly and Bingo.
"Rudolph?"

"Montgomery, that's you," said Woolma. "Have you learned your lines?"

"Of course," said Montgomery.

"Well, you don't have much to learn," said Zipper with a touch of envy. "There isn't much difference between a lead reindeer and a lead moose."

Everyone laughed.

Then Braker Turtle stood up and cleared his throat. "When the play is over, we are going to give the presents to the needy children. Then refreshments will be served. Lolly can tell you about them."

"My father is donating candy canes and popcorn balls for everyone," Lolly said.

"Good," said Montgomery. "What's happening with the costumes?"

"They're in that box on the shelf. I finished them yesterday," said Bernice. "We made a really great reindeer suit for you, Montgomery. But you have to bring your own antlers."

Montgomery blushed. "He's going to be the moost — I mean *most* — wonderful Rudolph ever," said Woolma. And everyone laughed again.

"Have I forgotten anything?" asked Montgomery.

Portia raised her hand. "You forgot my star. I made it out of silver foil for the top of the Christmas tree. It's in the chest with the presents."

Dotty was in charge of presents. She opened the lid of the chest and said proudly, "I want to report that we have more presents this year than ever before. Everyone in town has donated something for the needy children. Just look!"

"It looks like a whole lot of nothing to me," Rocco said.

Dotty glared at him. "That isn't funny," she said. "They are not *nothing*. They are beautiful presents."

"No, I mean it," said Rocco. "There's nothing there!"

Everyone looked in the chest.

"Why, they're gone!" gasped Dotty. "How can that be? I just put the last presents in here before lunch."

Bingo pulled out a note from the empty chest and read it aloud.
It said:

> I took the presents to the North Pole.
> Thanks for all your help, gang. See you
> on Christmas Eve.
>
> S. Claus

Everyone was horrified. "Santa Claus wouldn't do that," said Portia. "I know he wouldn't. He brings presents *from* the North Pole, not *to* the North Pole."

"Portia's right," said Dotty. "I think someone has taken the presents."

"I bet you hid them, Rocco," said Bingo.

"I did not," Rocco shot back. "You probably bet them — and lost!" Montgomery called for order, but the gang was too excited to listen.

"I'm going to tell Officer Growler," said Zipper, and in a flash he was out the door. Bingo ran after him. Portia started to cry.

"Let's all go," said Rudyard.

"Good idea," said Montgomery. "But first, let's look around here and see if anything else is missing."

Officer Growler was not in the police station when Zipper and Bingo burst through the door. Instead, his nephew Burymore Bloodhound was asleep at the desk.

"Where's Officer Growler?" shouted Zipper.

"Uh . . . he's not here," said Burymore, putting his feet on the floor. "He had to go someplace for an hour, so he made me his deputy. What can I do for you . . . uh . . . boys?"

"You can wake up! The presents are missing!" said Bingo.

"Presents? What presents?" yawned Burymore.

"The presents we were going to give to the orphans at the pageant tonight," said Bingo.

"They're not missing," said Burymore. "They're with the reindeer who was just pulling them around in a cart."

Zipper and Bingo were surprised. "A reindeer?" they said.

"Yes," said Burymore. "A reindeer with horns."

At that moment the rest of the gang burst into the police station. Burymore Bloodhound pointed his finger at Montgomery. "There's the reindeer with the horns," he said. "He has the presents."

Montgomery was flabbergasted. "I don't have any presents," he said. "They've been stolen. And so have the costumes."

Deputy Bloodhound kept his eyes on Montgomery. "Facts are facts. A reindeer was sighted in Green Meadow pulling a cart filled with presents. Who else in town fits the description — big feet, long nose, brown fur, and horns!"

"You're wrong!" said Bingo. "Montgomery wouldn't do such a thing." The rest of the gang shouted in agreement.

"Listen to what he is saying," Dotty told the deputy. "Our costumes have been stolen. And that includes the reindeer costume."

"Right," said Montgomery. "Someone is running around Green Meadow in *my* reindeer costume. And that someone is the Christmas thief."

"What are we going to do? We don't have much time," said Woolma.

"I think we need Officer Growler," cried Portia.

Montgomery straightened his shoulders. "I'm going to find the thief — and clear my name."

"Which direction did he go?" asked Bernice.

"Uh . . . toward Gummyfoot Swamp," said Burymore.

"Gummyfoot Swamp!" said Bingo. "That's where Catchum Crocodile and his creepy sidekick Leland live."

"Right," shouted the gang. "They stole our things!"

"We'll need evidence to prove it," said Montgomery grimly.
"Bernice, you come with me and look for clues. Together we should
be able to find them. The rest of you go back to the clubhouse
and start making presents. I don't want any kids to be disappointed."

"We'll do our best," said Dotty.

The snow was falling faster and faster as Montgomery and Bernice headed toward Gummyfoot Swamp. "It will be hard to see," said Montgomery.

"I have good eyes," said Bernice. To prove it, she pointed to a small tree. "Look! Someone has ripped the branches off that pretty tree!"

Montgomery examined it carefully, "Hmmmm," he said. "It looks like the kind of thing Catchum Crocodile would do. But what would he want with a bunch of branches?"

As they walked along, Bernice gave Montgomery instructions on how to scout. "You have to look up in the air and down on the ground," she said. Montgomery lifted his eyes to the sky.

"Hey, what's that?" he said, pointing up in a tree. Stuck in the branches was a silver star. To reach it, Bernice had to stand on Montgomery's shoulders.

"That's the star Portia made," she said excitedly. "Catchum probably just threw it away, and it landed in that tree." She put it carefully in her pocket.

"We're on the right track," said Montgomery. They hurried ahead.
"Look there!" shouted Bernice. "Another clue!" A beautiful doll
lay half-buried in the snow. Montgomery picked it up and put it
under his arm.

Up ahead they could see a light shining in a window. "That's
Catchum's hideaway," said Montgomery. "Let's go."

They ran quietly through the snow until they reached the house.
Outside was the empty cart that Catchum had used. Bernice and
Montgomery nodded silently to each other when they saw it and
drew up to the window.

Catchum stood among the presents, admiring himself in the mirror. He was still dressed in the reindeer suit. He turned left, then right, and kept touching the antlers on his head.

"Gee, Boss, you look great in that costume," said Leland. "It was a good idea to use those branches as antlers."

"What a great Christmas this is," said Catchum gleefully. "We have presents for the swamp rats, and we didn't spend a penny for them. The Get Along Gang's Christmas Pageant is ruined. And *I* am the perfect Rudolph!"

"You sure are, Boss," said Leland. "You should be playing the part. You look more like Rudolph than that moose ever could. Even if he were right in this room, I couldn't tell which of you was the real Rudolph."

Suddenly the door flew open. "You're not Rudolph," said
Montgomery. "You're nothing but a thief!"

Catchum was so scared that he shook. His antlers fell to the floor. "I just wanted presents for the swamp rats," he said. "We don't have money to buy any."

"Y-y-yeah," stammered Leland from under the table.

"That's no excuse," said Montgomery. "Lots of people don't have money and they don't steal. The swamp rats could have come to the pageant. We would have given them presents."

Catchum picked up the antlers. "But I want to be Rudolph in the pageant," he whined.

"Take that reindeer suit off right now," said Montgomery. "You're not going anywhere. And I'm warning you — you better not try to come to the pageant."

Catchum took off the costume. Then he and Leland watched Bernice and Montgomery pick up all the presents and put them in a neat pile by the door.

Bernice opened the door. "Oh, Montgomery, the snow is too
deep. We'll never be able to pull the cart with all the presents in it."

Montgomery thought for a minute. "I have an idea. We'll take Catchum after all. He'll use his tail to brush a path for us all the way to the clubhouse." He looked at the gloomy Catchum. "So get going."

Bernice walked alongside while Montgomery pulled the cart through the snow, yelling, "Faster, Catchum, faster!"

The snow flew to the sides as Catchum waved his tail back and forth.

Dotty saw them first. "They're here!" she shouted. "And Catchum is with them."

"We found the thief . . . and the presents too!" said Montgomery. The gang cheered. "Guess who the other reindeer was?" Everyone turned to Catchum.

"I'll watch him while the rest of you load up the other presents," said Zipper.

The gang quickly put the presents in the cart. Rocco and Bingo carried out the Christmas tree. But the cart was so full that Montgomery couldn't pull it.

"Let's push," said Rocco. "Together we can make it there."
The gang got behind the cart. Catchum took his place in front
and began to clear a path with his tail.

In no time, they arrived at the schoolhouse. Montgomery yelled, "We have thirty minutes to get ready."

Rocco and Bingo put up the tree. Woolma and Flora hung the decorations. Lolly strung lights around the room. Dotty put the chairs in neat rows. Braker fastened a big wreath on the door. Zipper put raisins and nuts in a bowl. Even Catchum and Leland helped. They started a fire in the fireplace. Everyone took the presents from the cart and put them under the tree.

Suddenly Portia began to cry. "My star. It's not here. You brought back everything except my star."

"I forgot," said Bernice. "It's in my pocket."

She took out the star and handed it to Portia. Portia beamed as she hung it on the tree.

Everyone changed into their costumes. From outside they heard
the sound of music, so they threw open the doors. The whole
town was walking toward the schoolhouse, carrying candles and
singing Christmas carols.

"Merry Christmas," shouted the Get Along Gang.

And Merry Christmas to you.